TWO GOOD EARS

TWO GOOD EARS

STORIES

Leah Browning

Silent Station Press

Published in the United States of America
by Silent Station Press.

Cover painting: *Marguerite*,
1903, oil on canvas, 117.5 x 73.7 cm
by William-Adolphe Bouguereau

Publisher's Cataloging-in-Publication Data

Browning, Leah
Two good ears: stories / Leah Browning
ISBN 978-0-578-31291-0
Short stories, American. | Short stories (single
author). | Domestic fiction.

CONTENTS

TWO GOOD EARS

THREADS

I was only five when a tiger bit off one of my hands.

My mother filled a glove with sand and sewed it to my stump. Every year, she cut the seam with a miniature pair of sewing scissors and stitched on a new glove.

Under my clothes, the skin of my arms and legs became a patchwork. A small pillow with a pattern of rosebuds took the place of a shoulder.

Dinnertime. My mother sent me outside with a bucket of raw meat.

With my remaining hand, I rang the bell. I waited as they walked toward me.

FRIDAY NIGHT AT THE MERMAID INN

Mary Lee hasn't slept in days. The hospital sent the baby to a NICU in the city and discharged Mary Lee after twenty-four hours. She's already back waiting tables. Fitz has been out of work for almost a year and she can't afford to lose this job.

All morning, she pours hot coffee and carries plates of pancakes out from the kitchen. After the lunch rush, she'll get a little break. Her calves are killing her, and the bottoms of her feet. She ran out of little corn pads but she doesn't want to ask Fitz to go to the drugstore and buy more.

When the man in the chambray work shirt puts down his napkin, Mary Lee takes the check to his table. She's waited on him a couple of times before. As she turns to walk away, he says, "When are you having your baby?"

Her stomach is still a round bulge under her uniform. "Soon," she says.

"Well, good luck," he tells her, and after he finishes with the cashier, Mary Lee sees him go back to the table and slip a twenty-dollar bill under the salt and pepper shakers.

When her shift is over, Fitz meets her out back, by the dumpster. He borrowed a car from one of their neighbors. A couple of years earlier, after his wife left him, the guy slept on their couch for a week. The first night, he and Fitz stayed up late talking, and from the bedroom, with the door closed, Mary Lee could hear him crying.

It's almost a two-hour drive to the hospital, and even with the windows open and the radio turned up loud, Mary Lee has trouble keeping her eyes open. "It's fine," Fitz says, but she's afraid to fall asleep.

It feels like a superstition, but if she doesn't keep an eye on things, maybe he will fall asleep at the wheel, or have an accident. Fitz is a careful driver, and yet. She just doesn't want to take any chances.

The motel, when they turn into the lot, is practically deserted. It's the off-season. They get a room with large sliding-glass windows overlooking the pool.

Fitz and Mary Lee wash their faces and undress and climb into bed. It's then, as she's dozing off, that her mind starts up again. Thinking of the baby is like touching an infected tooth. The wretchedness and fear radiate through her entire body.

They don't know, though. They don't know anything yet. All they can do is wait until morning and go where they're told.

Late that night, Mary Lee hears splashing from outside. She is half asleep. Fitz is sitting up beside her, watching television with the sound turned down. He's the type who can concentrate on anything.

Waves of light move across the white ceiling. She is half asleep, it is the middle of the night, and there is the ceiling or sky, the splashing. For a moment, lying there on her back, Mary Lee thinks that she is outside on the water. For a moment, she thinks that she is floating.

TWO GOOD EARS

We went to visit Wendy in the hospital. She had a big white bandage covering her ear. The dog had bitten off the bottom part of her earlobe. Her mother made a fuss over the flowers we brought and served us vanilla ice cream in little dishes. When we got back to the neighborhood, when we were alone again, it was all we could talk about.

A day or two later, Wendy came home. Our houses were newer builds, all unfenced, and she had been running down the long stretch of our shared backyard, her blond hair like long streamers behind her. She was the fastest runner in the entire fourth grade. The dog had leapt on her back and knocked her to the ground. We had all seen it.

The doctor stitched her up as best he could, but Wendy was still self-conscious about her ears. She stopped wearing ponytails and let the hole in her other ear close up. Sometimes, if one of us had something she wanted, she'd open her jewelry box and offer earrings in trade.

When we were thirteen, for Samantha's birthday, her parents let her throw a slumber party in their basement. Her birthday was right before Halloween, so we painted each other's nails black and watched scary movies. Most of the food was regular, but her mother had helped her fix Vienna sausages and catsup to look like severed fingers, and there was a huge bowl of fruit punch with plastic spiders frozen into the ice cubes.

At one o'clock in the morning, her dad came down and told us to switch off the lights and go to sleep. Then he went upstairs and left us alone again.

Someone suggested telling ghost stories, and someone else said that ghost stories were boring. We decided to play Truth or Dare.

The first few rounds were uninspired. Lick the floor, Who do you like?—that sort of thing. Then it was Samantha's turn. She chose Dare. We got the idea of piercing her ears.

There was a girl whose older sister had told her that you could do it with ice, a sewing needle, and a potato. Samantha licked her lips and looked from one face to another. She said that she didn't think there were any potatoes in the house. That was all right, we decided. We didn't need one.

We marked a black dot on each earlobe, and when her first ear seemed good and numb, the girl with the older sister tried to stick in the needle. At the last second, Samantha lost her nerve and jerked her head away. The needle punctured her earlobe, but nowhere near the black dot, and we had to wait for Samantha to stop thrashing before we could pull it out again.

Do you want me to do the other side? the girl with the sister asked. She held up the needle. A drop of blood fell on the carpet.

Are you crazy, Samantha said. She was trying not to let us see that she was crying.

We went to visit Samantha when she got home from the doctor. She'd been in bed with a fever for two days before she took off her hat and showed her mother the swollen, oozing ear.

She was sitting on a chair at the kitchen table. Her ear was loosely bandaged, and she looked terrible, flushed and misshapen. Her hair was stringy and flat in back from lying down for so long. We weren't sure what was going on under the gauze. Her ear could have turned black and fallen off, for all we knew. We were afraid to ask. So we each drank a glass of apple juice and chewed our nails.

On the way home, a woman jogged by with a dog on a leash, and Wendy ducked behind us. She was still afraid of dogs, even small ones.

When we were nine and that dog had leapt on Wendy's back and knocked her down, her mother had come flying out the back door of their house with a kitchen broom in her hand.

We turned seventeen, eighteen. That summer, for the last time, we worked at the ice cream parlor and pizzeria in our little town and then drove around until it was far too late, talking. At home we were tired, insolent. Our mothers stood with their hands on their hips and told us to clean our rooms and take out the trash. God gave you two good ears, they said. Why don't you ever use them?

But it was no use. We had floated so far away from them at that point that we couldn't hear a thing.

GRAVEL

The therapist said Brendan wanted me to be his mother. That's why he kept kicking little holes in the wall and pulling his own hair.

"I don't want to be his mother," I said. We'd been dating for four years. I felt like that went without saying.

"Well, that's what he's telling you with his behavior," she said smartly. This is the kind of smug insight I was paying $100 an hour for.

When I got home, Brendan was lying on his back on the bed. I could see his shirt and tie wadded up on the floor, where he had started throwing them every day when he got home from work. His heels were resting lightly on the wall.

A contractor had just spent two days repairing the drywall and painting over the damaged spots. The paint was too thin, I realized. Now that it had dried, I could still see where Brendan had drawn a big red apple and the words, "Bite me."

On closer inspection, though, it became obvious that he had just made the drawing again on top of the fresh paint. The same apple, the same words.

"I think we need to break up," I said.

"I think we need to break up," he repeated, high-pitched, imitating my voice.

"Stop it," I told him sternly. The therapist had said that I needed to be more forceful.

He made a face. "Stop it," he whined.

We were supposed to be at a Christmas party in two hours.

I pointed at the clock. "Get dressed," I said.

"Make me," he said.

*　*　*

I parked at the bottom of the hill. It was dark, spooky, out here where all the trees pointed their long, bony fingers in our direction.

Brendan was slumped down in his seat. He'd spent the entire drive flipping the car radio from one station to another. I could feel a dull headache coming on.

On both sides of the long driveway, all the way up to the house, our hosts had placed small paper bags, each filled with sand and a lit candle.

We walked in between the luminarias. Gravel crunched under our boots.

Every time I looked up at the top of the hill, I could see the house, glowing through the trees like a symbol of all that is fine and beautiful in the world.

Out of the corner of my eye, I saw Brendan fumble with something.

I sighed. I was so exasperated by this point. "What's in your mouth?" I asked.

He didn't answer, though—just went on chewing.

I stopped walking and unbuttoned my coat. "Hey, look, dummy," I said. "I can do it too." I picked up a bit of gravel and put it in my mouth. It tasted dirty and gritty and surprisingly satisfying.

Brendan shifted a stone into his cheek. "Spit that out," he said.

I smirked. "You look like a chipmunk."

"You do."

"No, you do."

He put his arm around me.

As we walked up the front steps, we could hear music and laughter.

"Ring the doorbell," I said.

"No, you ring it."

We had reached an impasse.

15

When I thought about it, I was also tired of mopping the kitchen floor and paying bills.

Inside the house, people were growing old and dying, but as long as we stood on the porch, on the periphery, we could stay exactly as we were.

Brendan didn't look at me. "Let's go back down the hill and start again," he said. "We can come right back."

Who knew what would happen next? So I agreed. We spat out our rocks, seeing who could spit farther. They made little holes in the snow and disappeared. It might have been the first time I'd seen him smile in weeks.

Then he took my hand, and for at least a few minutes, we were just two children, running through the forest.

SMALL TALK

Paulie decided, as a joke, to buy a gorgeous, formerly handfed Scarlet Macaw. She put the parrot in a tall gilt birdcage in the corner of her living room, where it could be seen from the front window, provided that the drapes were open.

She invited her friends over for drinks. They poked their fingers in between the bars of the cage until the parrot fanned its tail feathers.

"Say Paulie," Paulie said.

The bird said nothing.

"Maybe he's a mute," one of her friends said teasingly, and the others laughed.

Paulie's cheeks began to burn.

After they had left, and for months afterward, Paulie stood next to the cage and repeated her name, but no matter how she tried to goad the bird into speaking, it would not.

She invited her friends over for a dinner party.

As a housewarming gift, her parents had bought her an antique dining room table, dishes, linen napkins, and every kind of drinking glass imaginable. She set the table with flowers and tall tapered candles. She unlocked the front door.

All afternoon, she had felt weak, parched, as though she were shriveling into a small dry husk.

In the corner, the bird was plucking its feathers. Its dish was empty again.

If it was hungry enough, Paulie thought, maybe it would do a trick.

This had not worked in the past, but nevertheless, she held out her hand, offering the bird a bit of seed.

Instead of taking the seed, it bit her finger, snapping it off and swallowing it in one quick gulp. Paulie watched in horror as the bird slipped its beak back out and bit down on what was left of her hand, then her arm.

By the time her friends arrived, she was caught in the bird's throat. They placed their bottles of wine on the sideboard and admired Paulie's table setting.

Her friends gathered in the living room, waiting for the food to be delivered.

She tried to get their attention. "Paulie," she croaked.

Someone laughed delightedly and said, "It learned how to talk!" Paulie heard footsteps. She could only manage to rasp out her own name, though, over and over. The friend who had approached the cage soon lost interest and drifted back to the group.

One of the women had misunderstood the invitation and brought her boyfriend. They arrived late, with a six-pack, and let themselves in.

The boyfriend nodded as he was introduced around. He felt out of place. When he thought no one would notice, he escaped. Standing at the kitchen counter, he drank three beers, then wandered into the living room again.

The women had already moved over to the dining table and sat down, pushing the plates and napkins aside. They were drinking white wine and talking about going to Italy on a group vacation.

Now that Paulie's friends were no longer in the way, the boyfriend noticed the macaw, standing motionless in the birdcage in the corner of the living room. Paulie had pulled the drapes in preparation for the party, and he couldn't make it out very well. He walked closer.

"Hey birdie," he said.

It didn't move.

"I'm talking to you, bird," he said. "Say something."

When it did not, he rattled the cage. "Come on. Talk."

The parrot shifted slightly on its perch.

"Say, 'I'm a stupid parrot,'" the man said. He tucked his arms up in a rough imitation of wings. "Say, 'I'm a bird and I can't even fly.' Say it."

Behind him, he could hear faint conversation and a woman's laughter.

He leaned toward the cage and wrapped his fingers around the bars. "If you were my bird, I would *make* you talk," he said.

The parrot watched, silent, its little eyes glittering in the low light.

PAINTED LADIES

We bought a late 1880s Victorian in San Francisco for 2.5 million dollars. That year, we posed for our Christmas card in the front parlor by the wood-burning fireplace.

First she was laid off, then I was. I bought a new tube of lipstick and two button-down shirts. Every day, we woke up early and went on interviews.

At home, I could feel a draft from the bay window and the sink in the powder room leaked. Mortgage payments had been coming out of our savings account for months. We couldn't afford to have anything repaired.

She wasn't back yet. I took off my shoes and walked through the rooms. No one was calling. The house was so quiet it echoed.

That morning, a man in a three-piece suit had looked up from my résumé and asked why I had submitted an application when I was so overqualified. I had smiled serenely before I answered.

I wiped off my makeup. There was no organic food left in the kitchen. We had already sold most of our furniture. I lay down on the wide-plank French oak floors and looked up at the sky.

TIEBREAKERS

They held David's funeral at our grandmother's church in Albuquerque. She was the one who placed a notice in the newspaper and had his body transported back from Kentucky after the motorcycle accident. He was only twenty-eight when he died.

This was years ago. You may have been there yourself, if you knew him. He was the one who had lost his leg in an earlier accident. He used to hop up and down the stairs of our house on his real leg, which always made my heart catch in my throat, but he used the prosthetic when he was on a level surface. If he was wearing jeans, it just looked like he had a minor limp.

All during the service, a heavyset man in a brown suit sat at the back of the church and mopped his eyes with a handkerchief. No one recognized him at first, or at least, I don't think they did. They hadn't seen him since David was a little boy.

The part you'd remember was later, at the gravesite. The man threw himself on the coffin and sobbed. If we had all lowered him into the empty hole in the ground and shoveled dirt onto him, you could just tell, he would have willingly let it happen. At the time, it was the worst thing I'd ever seen.

After he'd worn himself out crying, a couple of the men from the funeral home helped him up off the coffin and led him away.

That was David's stepfather, my aunt told me on the way to the reception. I already knew the rest of the story. David was only four years old when his mother died in a car accident. She would have been my aunt, too, but I had never known her. When David's mother died his stepfather didn't want him anymore. David had to move back in with his father, who was a notorious drunk.

The stepfather blamed himself for what had happened, my aunt said. The missing leg, the drinking, all the drugs. Poor David, she added, shaking her head. He'd gotten mixed up in some things.

The following year, my mother got married. She'd been living with my father for years, calling him her husband, but he'd only just gotten divorced from his first wife.

They moved all the furniture back and got married in our living room. My grandmother sat on an ottoman with a big corsage pinned to the front of her dress. She cried and cried. I knelt on the floor next to her and held her hand. Why are you crying, I asked.

Don't worry. I'm just happy. They're happy tears, she said, though I could see that she wasn't, and they weren't.

Once, I overheard my mother telling her girlfriends about a Christmas party she'd been to with my father. A woman they'd never met had arrived late, at the top of the stairs, in a long red dress. It was quite the entrance, my mother said. He saw her across the room, and he fell head over heels in love with her.

When they got home that night, they'd both been drunk, and my mother screamed and threw an empty bottle at my father, but when she told her girlfriends the story, it was just a big joke. She left those parts out.

Her friends smiled and nodded politely, but they didn't laugh. They'd heard other versions of this joke, and they already knew the punch line.

When I turned eighteen, I flew to Orlando. Every semester, my father sent me a check to pay for school, and I used the money to buy a two-bedroom condo with an outdoor patio and access to a community pool. I worked part-time at a copy shop and watched cartoons on my days off.

My father didn't catch on until it was time to graduate. When he called me, I said I'd never felt like he loved me as much as he loved the kids he had with his first wife. They were almost as old as my mother and I'd never even met them. He accused me of trying to manipulate him. I said, Well, I learned from the best, and he hung up on me.

I put the phone back in its cradle. The fan whirred overhead. A short time later, the telephone rang again. This time, it would have been my mother. I let it go to voicemail. I sat on the couch and looked around at all my pretty things.

After every breakup, I took a souvenir. Sometimes it was a pair of mugs, or a book, or a little figurine. Sometimes something bigger: a painting, or a piece of furniture. I had a lot of photographs and a drawer full of costume jewelry.

The last guy I'd gone home with had been a geology major. One night, lying in bed, he'd traced his finger over my bare shoulder and talked about strata. He said, The more you dig, the more layers there are. And he was right; there's always more to the story. His bomber jacket was hanging in the hall closet next to dresses from every girl I'd ever known.

In my pocket was a Zippo lighter they'd found in David's pocket when he died. I flicked it open and ran my thumb along the wheel. Heads I will, tails I won't, I

29

thought, though none of it made any sense.

On the table next to me, the phone rang and rang.

ADRENALINE

In the middle of the night, Jeff had a heart attack and Shayla rode in the ambulance next to him, holding his gray hand, adrenaline surging through her body so she almost couldn't breathe and the siren screaming above them as they raced through the dark toward the doctor who would press hard with his gloved hands on the body that she no longer recognized while Shayla sat in this bright fluorescent waiting room with its plastic chairs and piles of magazines with those vacuous celebrity faces smiling or looking down their noses even though they were the ones choosing to stand in a room full of strangers with their clothes off, and Shayla knew that this was the worst thing that had ever happened to her; she thought with

31

dread of calling Jeff's mother and sister and telling them what had happened and hearing them cry, but there was also a tiny thought in the back of her mind that when this was all over maybe she could find another man who didn't drink as much and didn't get into trouble at work and didn't want to wait another year to have a baby even though Shayla had been waiting six years already and maybe then she could finally be happy, but then the doctor came out and smiled and smiled and shook her hand and said what a relief this must be.

SUSPENSION

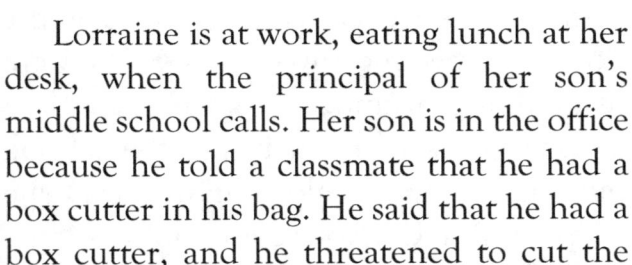

Lorraine is at work, eating lunch at her desk, when the principal of her son's middle school calls. Her son is in the office because he told a classmate that he had a box cutter in his bag. He said that he had a box cutter, and he threatened to cut the other boy's face off with it.

You need to come pick him up, the principal says.

School personnel emptied the bag, and Lorraine's son didn't actually have any weapons at all. Even his pencils were dull. Still, he's being suspended for two days.

Lorraine drives the speed limit on the way to the school. A vein is pulsing in her temple. This is the fourth time she's gotten a call from one of the boys' schools in the past month. She's had to leave her office

33

during a work day before, but this is the first time any of them have been suspended.

I was kidding, he tells her in the principal's office. He's looking down at the floor, not meeting anyone's eyes. We were just kidding around.

She keeps it down inside the school, but once they are alone in the car, she snaps at him. Use your common sense, she says. Would you, just as a joke, tell a security guard at the airport that you have a bomb in your bag? Well, would you?

The color is high in his cheeks. Um, no? he says.

Of course not, she says. They have to take these things seriously.

At home, Lorraine sends him to his room. She's getting a tension headache. What is she going to do with him for the next two days? She has a report due in the morning, and the messages are piling up in her inbox.

And where is Joe? He's in California, clearing his head. He has a girlfriend now. The woman is a few years older than Lorraine, but she's not saddled with children so she still has time to go to the salon and get her roots colored. They do yoga and have a champagne brunch every Saturday, Joe told Lorraine last time they talked.

When they were twenty, Lorraine couldn't imagine anything in the world she wanted more than to marry Joe and have babies with him. Now, she just wants to kill him.

Not literally, of course. It's a figure of speech, isn't it?

Even in her thoughts, she can't stop explaining, making excuses. Don't worry, she wants to say—she doesn't really want to kill anyone. She was just kidding around.

The room is empty, though, and she has no one to tell.

CIRCUITRY

In the fall of 1952, when I was eight years old, my mother lay down on the couch in the living room. For the next six months, she rarely got up again.

I was able to keep this secret for a long time because no one was around to notice. Although my parents had never formally divorced, my father rented a two-room apartment in a nearby town. He owned a furniture store there, and he told me that he liked to keep tabs on it. When I asked him what he did every night, he said that he ate at the diner nearby or swam laps in the community pool.

He visited on the weekends, sometimes, and I started to meet him on the front steps, wearing a dress with a pinafore I had starched myself. My hair was badly braided, but he didn't seem to notice, only placing a hand on the back of my head with a fond, distracted smile.

The front door of our house led right into the living room, and I was always afraid that he would open it and discover the scene inside. But things between my parents were often tense, and I think he was relieved that he didn't have to go in and try to make polite conversation with my mother.

Instead, we went out for an ice cream cone or some other little treat, and then he delivered me back to the house, waving from the car as I slipped inside.

This was on the occasional weekend, though. Most days, I saw only my mother.

She was stretched out on the living room couch, which was a faint green—a boxy shape, but not uncomfortable. At night, after I had changed out of my school clothes and finished doing math problems at the kitchen table, after I had cooked a dinner of scrambled eggs or cheese slipped between two slices of toasted bread, after I had rinsed and wiped the dishes and placed them back in the cupboard, I turned on the television and sat on the couch near my mother, folded into the crook of her knees. Once a week, I watched the Lone Ranger gaze into the distance, his hand on the neck of his horse.

That spring, someone from the school office got hold of my father, and as I left Mrs. Taylor's classroom and crossed the school's front lawn on my way home that afternoon, I saw him leaning against his car, waiting for me.

"Who's minding the store?" I asked.

He didn't answer, just opened the car door and waved me in. I climbed inside.

"Why are you here?"

Again, there was no reply. He drove me to my mother's house and parked in the driveway rather than alongside the curb, as he had taken to doing.

Suddenly, I could see everything that was wrong: the lawn gone to seed, the paint peeling off the shutters, the flowers that had long since died in their beds. Winter had softened these edges, but now that the light blanket of snow had melted, everything I had kept so carefully hidden had been exposed.

My mother was already gone. We didn't speak about this. I changed my clothes and did my homework, and at an appropriate time my father made me a peanut butter sandwich and an apple. I had just done the shopping and everything in the refrigerator was fresh.

Whenever I saw him, my father would give me a bit of money—twenty dollars, say, or twenty-five. Presumably he gave it because he felt guilty, but I didn't think about that. For months I had been making that occasional weekend money stretch out to cover all of our basic necessities. The women at the market would smile when they saw me take out my little change purse to pay for milk or toothpaste. My father was still paying our bills every month, so we never had to do without water, or electricity.

Many weeks later, I came home from school and found that my mother was back from the hospital. She met me at the door holding a spatula and wearing a red and white half apron with a ruffle along the bottom. She was baking cookies.

I thought that maybe this time, the treatments had worked. Now she could be a regular mother who threw birthday parties and made me eat my vegetables. My father, who was sitting on a chair in the living room staring into space, could sell his little apartment and move back into their bedroom on a permanent basis.

That night, though, he put his shoes back on and drove away. Briefly, he cupped the back of my head with his hand before he left.

She was standing in the kitchen, wearing dish gloves and holding a sponge. "Where is the soap?" she asked, though I had already answered the same question twice that afternoon. I pulled the bottle from the back of the sink to the front.

In the fall of 1987, when I was forty-three, my first boyfriend died. The obituary made no mention of AIDS; it said only that he had died after a prolonged illness.

My mother was the one who called and read the newspaper column to me over the phone. "It's so sad," she said. He had grown up just down the street from us, in the yellow house on the corner.

I knew then, as I had always known, that one day the phone call would be about her. All that afternoon, for hours after I hung up the phone, I couldn't seem to stop crying.

At dinnertime, my daughter called. She had just gotten home from work and was trying to make meatballs. What do you add to the ground beef, she wanted to know. She had moved into her first real apartment the year before, and her younger brother, my son, was in his last year of college.

I wiped my face on my sleeve. "Do you have saltines?" I asked, and waited on the line while she checked her pantry.

THE LEMON SEED

Every morning, after she finished her breakfast, Ilana swallowed a lemon seed. She did it furtively, waiting until her mother had taken the teacups and plates to the kitchen. Then, from her pocket, Ilana withdrew the white seed and closed her eyes. Every day she wished that a lemon tree would grow inside her. Every day, she swallowed the pill, made the wish, and nothing happened. It didn't work and it didn't work.

Until, suddenly, it did.

As she lay in bed one night, Ilana could feel something, just a hint of green unfolding, ever so slowly, in the space below her ribcage.

She could scarcely breathe, not wanting to shift or draw attention to herself, and in the months and years that followed, she carried her body carefully through the house, then through the hallways at school. She walked close to walls and kept her eyes down. Miniature lemons were nested, now, in the narrow pathways between her heart and lungs.

Ilana got older, taller, but the lemon tree began to outpace her body. Some days, the pain was almost unbearable. As a young girl, she had imagined only a graceful branch, a few pieces of fruit that she could share. Instead, the limbs grew increasingly dense inside her, extending along the bones of her arms. She could follow the path of one or another as they spread along her internal scaffolding, aware of the scrape against bone, the intense, knotty pressure at the knuckles, and then the ends of the branches pushing up against the soft pad of flesh at the end of each finger, pressing up and out, as leaves unfurled just under the tips of her nails.

No one was able to eat the lemons, either, as it turned out. Even her mother, who cut lemons for every piece of fish and bowl of salad, continued to buy them at the market. There was something too odd about eating a piece of fruit that Ilana had grown in her own body.

She was able to hold down a steady job for the first few years out of school. She taught language classes, wearing long sleeves and trimming her branches enough that she could manage the chalk. Her limbs seemed chunky and malformed under her sweaters, but the students were new to the country and didn't ask questions. They repeated after her: I grow, you grow, he/she/it grows, we grow, they grow. I grew. I have grown. I am growing.

By the time she was twenty-five, she could no longer drive a car or turn pages in a book. Ilana had to move back in with her mother, who made room first on the fold-out couch in the living room, then on the three-season porch, then in the garden, near the lilacs.

In the afternoons, her mother came outside to keep her company. She brought a book and a glass of iced tea, and sat on a lawn chair beside her.

At first, Ilana was angry, grief-stricken. She could no longer eat or walk or form words. But little by little, she forgot food and exercise and speech. She forgot everything she had lost. She knew only the fresh air, the wind, each light touch against the tips of her hair and leaves. The rich black soil surrounding her feet, and from them, the pale tapered ends of her roots. The sun on her face and shoulders and branches, and her mother's quiet presence, and then also the lemons themselves, expanding, filling her up.

ACKNOWLEDGMENTS

Grateful acknowledgment is made to the editors of the following publications in which these stories first appeared, sometimes in slightly different form:

Bellows American Review: "Tiebreakers"
Fiction Southeast: "Small Talk"
First Class Literary Magazine: "Threads"
Flash Flash Click: "Adrenaline"
Helen Literary Magazine: "Painted Ladies"
The Homestead Review: "Two Good Ears"
Newfound: "Friday Night at the Mermaid Inn"
Toad: "Gravel"

"The Lemon Seed" was first published in *Myth+Magic*, a limited edition anthology from *Sugared Water* and Porkbelly Press. "Circuitry" first appeared in *Field Notes*, a project of *Cordella Magazine*.

www.ingramcontent.com/pod-product-compliance
Lightning Source LLC
Chambersburg PA
CBHW060236180626
46813CB00007B/3116